MEDICI BOOKS FOR CHILDREN

Tom and the Mag Rainbow

written and illustrated
by
Jean Gilder

Tom was a very handsome badger, and a rather unusual one too, for the stripes on his face were white on black instead of the other way round. He was a very friendly badger, and when he moved into his new home he was looking forward to meeting his new neighbours. He soon met Mrs Bunny and her family, Gilla the squirrel, Old Toby Mole, and Kitty Badger, whom he especially liked.

One rainy day, as he was carrying some logs in for the fire, he bumped into someone very prickly. "Why can't you watch where you're going?" said a cross voice. "I'm very sorry", said Tom "I didn't see you—I think I was trying to carry too many logs," he laughed. "Well, hurry up and finish moving in, you are making the path all muddy," muttered the grumpy hedgehog, hurrying off with her prickles sticking out all over.

Tom Badger watched her go into the woods and sighed. "What did I do wrong?" he murmured to himself. "Nothing really, Lupin's always like that", said Gilla squirrel from a nearby tree. "We can't make her happy, so we just leave her alone."

Tom was relieved to know that he hadn't upset her, but he felt rather sorry for Lupin Hedgehog and wondered why she was so often cross.

Although Tom liked his new home, he thought his neighbours were not very happy, and he wished he could cheer them up. He noticed, too, that the cows in the farmer's meadow looked thin and hungry—there was hardly any grass for them to eat.

Now Tom had brought a sack of wheat with him, which he had gleaned from a field after the crop had been harvested. He needed to have it ground into flour, so that he could make bread.

One morning the rain cleared a little and he suddenly saw there was a windmill perched up on a hill not too far away. So he slung the sack of wheat onto his shoulders and set off in the direction of the mill. Tom decided he would make himself feel more cheerful by pretending he was happy and, as he trudged along, he whistled a tune.

Presently a watery sun broke through the clouds and, looking up, Tom saw a beautiful rainbow arching across the sky. He stopped in surprise, for the end of it seemed to go right in through a little window high up in the windmill.

When Tom reached the mill, he pushed open the door and started to climb the rather dark, cobwebby ladder, carrying his sack of wheat. As he climbed up and up, he became aware of a quavery voice chanting a strange song:

"To work the mill
  And cast my spell
With nature's help
  I love so well . . .
To turn sorrow and pain
  And endless rain
(Through one good soul
  Who comes now near)
To love and laughter
  Sun and cheer . . . ."

Tom climbed the last steps rather wearily, and the singing suddenly ceased. "Come on up, Tom Badger", said the voice, and Tom, wondering how the Miller knew his name, popped his head through the trap door.

Dazzling light flooded the room in many lovely colours, and Tom blinked in surprise.

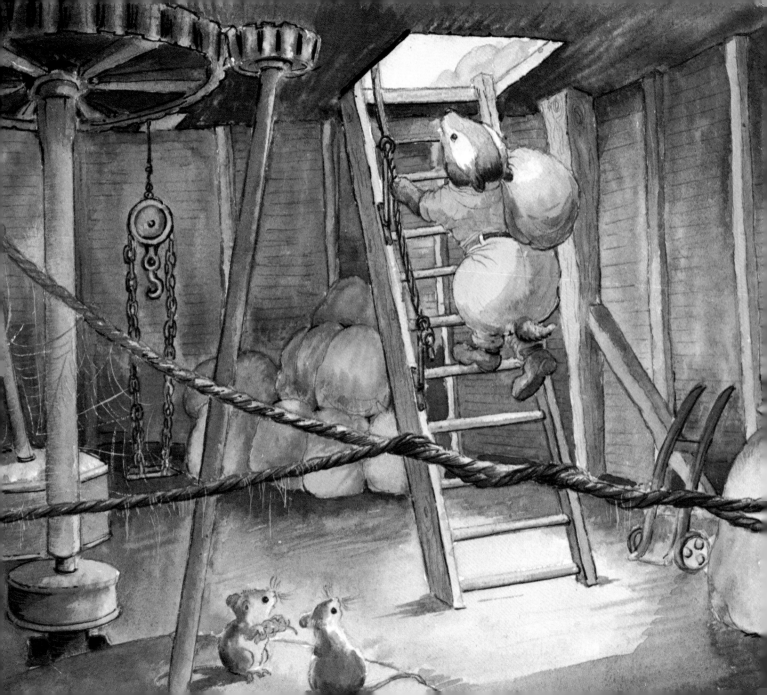

Tom watched in amazement as a strange little man took some empty cans and let them fill up with what looked like paint, as they caught the many colours of the rainbow all shimmering and sparkling.

"It isn't often that I can get my paint from a magic rainbow like this", said the Miller, "but now I must get back to my usual work."

He started up the mill machinery, tipped sack after sack into the hopper to feed the grindstones, and bagged up the flour as it came out. The Miller seemed to be getting quite tired, so Tom said, "Can I help you?" The Miller showed him what to do and together they worked hard.

At last all the wheat was ground, including the sack Tom had brought. They both sat down to a well-earned cup of mint tea.

"Well, Tom Badger, that was a good afternoon's work. Here is your flour, and something extra too, for helping me so kindly."

He presented the badger with seven of the tins, which now had tight-fitting lids.

"This is rather a special paint, Tom", he said. "I don't give this away very often—be careful how you use it."

"Thank you very much," said Tom happily, "now I must be getting back."

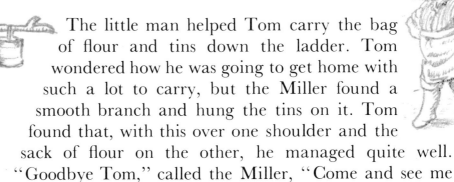

The little man helped Tom carry the bag of flour and tins down the ladder. Tom wondered how he was going to get home with such a lot to carry, but the Miller found a smooth branch and hung the tins on it. Tom found that, with this over one shoulder and the sack of flour on the other, he managed quite well. "Goodbye Tom," called the Miller, "Come and see me again one day."

As Tom walked away he looked back over his shoulder, but the rainbow was gradually fading, and the mill was quiet and dark.

The next day dawned dry but grey, and he decided to give Mrs Bunny a nice surprise, so whilst she was out he started painting her front door a lovely shade of blue. Tom worked away happily, and, when he had finished, stepped back to admire his work. The fresh blue paint looked extremely smart. Just then Mrs Bunny returned and was delighted to see what Tom had done.

They noticed the sky had almost cleared, and was a lovely blue.

Then he painted Toby Mole's fence bright yellow, and, as he finished, the sun peeped out from behind a cloud and shone a warm dazzling yellow.

Lupin Hedgehog came past with her shopping basket saying to Tom, "Huh, I suppose you think you're going to paint my house next—well I like it the way it is, thank you" and she shuffled off with a frown.

"Well, that's one less to bother with, anyway," murmured Tom to no one in particular.

Next he painted Gilla Squirrel's rain barrel a gay red, and as he worked he could hear faint popping noises—when he looked round . . . what a surprise! The poppies, which had been in tight bud, were bursting open, and all round him their scarlet silky flowers were nodding and swaying in the breeze.

After that, Tom chose a pretty pink for Kitty Badger's window frames. She was so pleased that she came tripping out and planted a kiss on Tom's painty cheek—he blushed even more pink.

The next day Tom was eager to try his wonderful paint again. The Dormice's flats looked bedraggled, so he painted all their doors and window frames a nice bright green— but this time he could not see anything different around him, and Tom was disappointed.

But as he passed the meadows on his way home, he suddenly noticed that the meadow was bright green with lush grass and the cows were munching away very contentedly.

Tom now had only orange and purple paint left; so he painted all his friends' garden tools and wheelbarrows with orange stripes and spots . . . and presently the sound of birdsong filled the air—two orange breasted robins were vying with each other to see who could sing the sweetest and loudest.

Tom scratched his head in puzzlement—what could he do with the purple paint? Everyone had new paint by now.

Then he had a good idea . . . the farmer's back door needed painting; so that night, when all was quiet, he tip-toed up with his brush and paint and carefully painted the door. But he could only reach half way up.

"Never mind, that looks better than nothing," he murmured to himself rather uncertainly.

As dawn broke, Tom hid in the bushes, waiting to see the pleased expression on the farmer's face.

But when the farmer opened the door and stuck to the paint—he didn't seem to be pleased at all.

In fact, his face turned a peculiar shade of purple.

Tom suddenly decided it was time to go.

By now, most of the paint had been used up, but there was a little of each colour left. After pondering for a while Tom had an idea—and he went to call on Lupin Hedgehog.

Tom knocked on her door. Lupin pulled back the bolts and poked her head out.

"Well, what do you want?" she snapped.

"I have some paint left, Lupin; I thought you might like to use it," said Tom.

"Hmm, I don't want a lot of messy old paints, thank you; you'd better take them away," replied Lupin crossly.

But Tom saw that the crotchety hedgehog was looking at the paints with some interest, so he left them outside her door.

The next day, the paints had gone, and there was no sign of Lupin for several days after that.

Toby Mole claimed that he had heard her *singing*— but nobody quite believed him; but when Gilla Squirrel knocked on her window to enquire if she was well, the window was flung open and Gilla was astonished to see a happy smiling Lupin.

"What have you been up to?" enquired Gilla.

"Come in, come in and see!" declared Lupin gaily.

Gilla went into her little front room and was amazed to see that the little hedgehog had been painting lots of tiny pictures of butterflies, acorns, caterpillars, toadstools, and so on.

"Oh Lupin, they are lovely," exclaimed Gilla, running to tell the other animals.

Well, they all crowded in to see the paintings, and thought Lupin was very clever.

Lupin blushed quite modestly at all the praise. Suddenly she said, "It's all due to Tom Badger, and oh dear . . . I've been so rude to him."

Lupin bustled round finding her shoes and coat. "I must see him now," she muttered. Then she lined up the paintings and asked the animals which they thought was the best one. They eventually chose her painting of a butterfly, with rainbow coloured wings.

Tom was most surprised when Lupin turned up on his doorstep and presented him with the lovely painting. "For your new home, Tom. I hope you'll be very happy living here with us," she said graciously.

"Why, thank you, Lupin, I'm sure I shall—this seems a *very* nice place to live, after all."